JERDINE NOLEN

Plantzilla

Illustrated by

DAVID CATROW

VOYAGER BOOKS
HARCOURT, INC.
Orlando Austin New York San Diego London

First Voyager Books edition 2005
VOYAGER BOOKS is a trademark of Harcourt, Inc., registered in the United States of America and/or
other jurisdictions.

The Library of Congress has cataloged the hardcover edition as follows:
Nolen, Jerdine.
Plantzilla/Jerdine Nolen; illustrated by David Catrow.
p. cm.
Summary: In a series of letters a boy, his science teacher, and his parents discuss the progress of a very
unusual, sometimes frightening plant that becomes more human as the summer progresses.
[1. Plants—Fiction. 2. Letters—Fiction. 3. Humorous stories.] I. Catrow, David, ill. II. Title.
PZ7.N723Pl 2002
[Fic]—dc21   2001004788
ISBN 978-0-15-202412-3
ISBN 978-0-15-205392-5 pb

TWP   12 11 10 9 8 7 6
4500221266

The illustrations in this book were done in watercolor and pencil.
Mortimer's and Mrs. Henryson's handwriting was created by Annie Cicale.
The display type was set in Rezin.
The text type was set in Typewriter.
Color separations by Bright Arts Ltd., Hong Kong
Printed and bound by Tien Wah Press, Singapore
Production supervision by Ginger Boyer
Designed by Judythe Sieck and Linda Lockowitz

For Matthew, the inspiration
—J. N.

For Deborah, who knows a good story
when she sees one
—D. C.

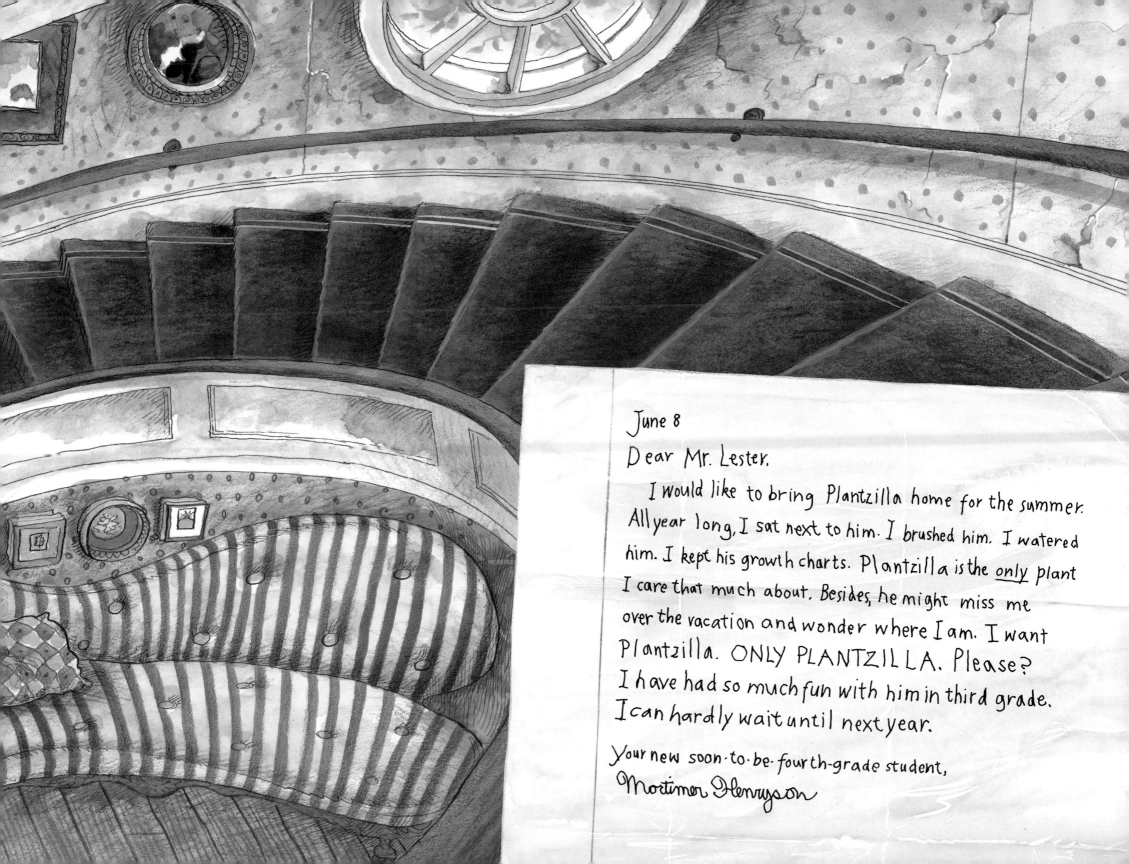

June 8

Dear Mr. Lester,

I would like to bring Plantzilla home for the summer. All year long, I sat next to him. I brushed him. I watered him. I kept his growth charts. Plantzilla is the <u>only</u> plant I care that much about. Besides, he might miss me over the vacation and wonder where I am. I want Plantzilla. ONLY PLANTZILLA. Please? I have had so much fun with him in third grade. I can hardly wait until next year.

Your new soon-to-be-fourth-grade student,

Mortimer Henryson

8 June

To Whom It May Concern:

Mortimer Henryson has permission to bring home a plant over summer vacation. We are happy to provide the care a plant would need to grow and thrive, as much sunlight does pour in through our windows. And there is more than enough water flowing from our clear crystal springs.

We will be breathing a little easier now with all that _extra_ oxygen. Don't you think this makes for the best kind of sym_biotic_ relationship? ··

Very truly yours,
Mr. & Mrs. Henry Henryson

P.S. Mortimer does have his heart set on one plant in particular. He called it Plantzilla. Do I have that right? It does seem like an odd name for a plant.

June 9

Dear Mr. & Mrs. Henryson,

I am delighted Mortimer has chosen Plantcilia. The plants were named based on their characteristics. The children nicknamed this one "Plantzilla" because "zilla" sounds like "cilia." As you are probably aware, cilia is a term used in botany to describe a hairlike material that can run along the margin or edge of a structure, such as a leaf, usually forming a fringe.

Mortimer has taken charge of Plantcilia's care and development. I am sure he will want to continue this over the summer. Of course, there are cases where the fondness for these plants grows as well. Don't be surprised if you find it difficult to part with Plantcilia at summer's end. If this should happen, I am happy to tell you that adoption is not out of the question!

Feel free to write or have Mortimer drop me a postcard if any questions should crop up, or just let me know how things are going. My address is:

Samuel G. Lester
c/o Plantimonium Holiday Aloha Resort
Honolulu, Hawaii

Very truly yours,
Samuel G. Lester
Science Teacher and Plant Program Coordinator
Strewbrick's Day School

P.S. Please be so kind and provide transportation for Plantcilia. These plants are not allowed on the bus.

June 15

Dear Mr. Lester,

Thank you for Plantzilla. Things are really going great! Plantzilla loves living here. I can tell. I just knew he would be happy. Remember when you said, "Different plants have different growing preferences"? That is _so_ true. Wait until you see how Plantzilla is growing.

The best news of all is that Plantzilla is beginning to eat _real_ food, mostly meat. I'll keep my notes up and will write again soon.

Your student,

Mortimer H.

June 25

Dear Mr. Lester,

Remember when you told us, "Caring for plants in this program gives you more benefits than you could ever imagine"? That is so true! Plantzilla is _so_ amazing! Wait until you see him. It's like he's more than alive.

Sometimes all I want to do is water him, brush his hairs, and watch him grow. He seems to like it when I loosen the soil around the top of his pot. I could watch him all day. But Mother says I should be running around and playing outside. I wish I could bring Plantzilla along. To me he's more than just a plant.

Thank you so much for giving me the chance to show you how I can _really_ care for Plantzilla. You may not even recognize him anymore! I love Plantzilla.

Your friend,
Mortimer H.

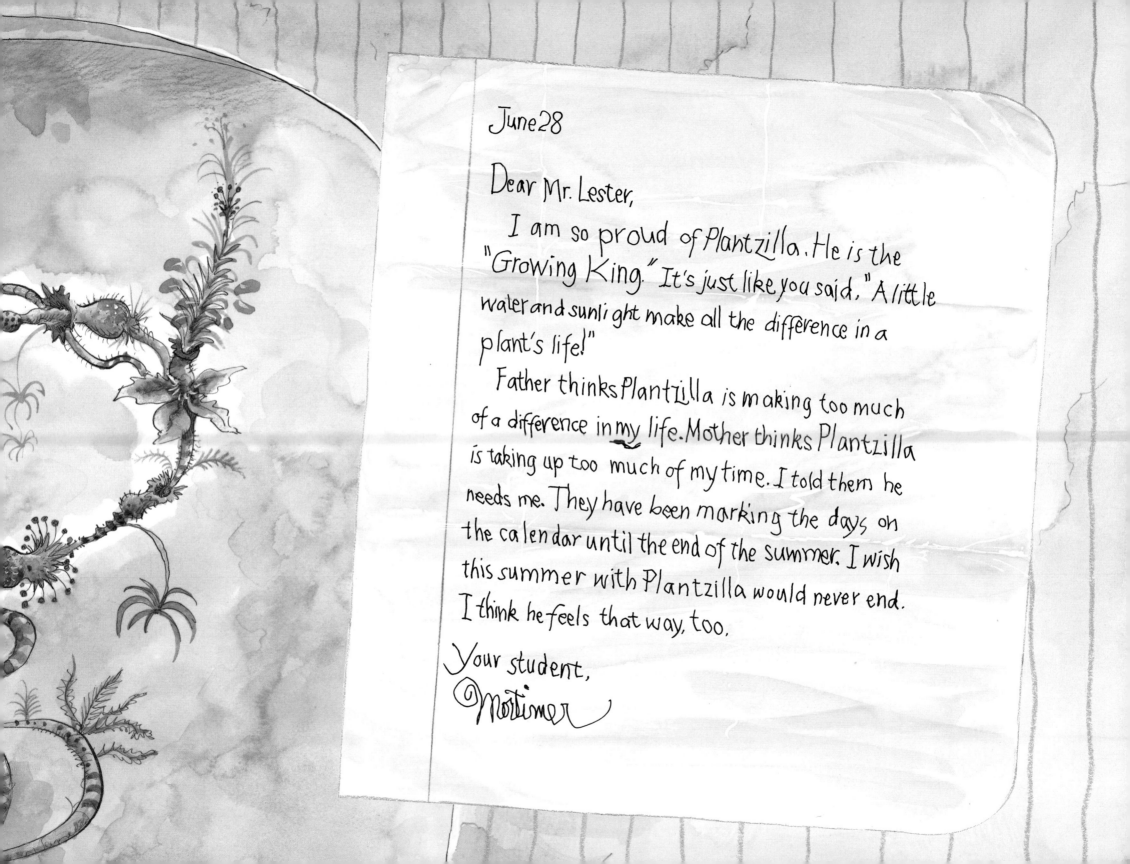

June 28

Dear Mr. Lester,

I am so proud of Plantzilla. He is the "Growing King." It's just like you said, "A little water and sunlight make all the difference in a plant's life!"

Father thinks Plantzilla is making too much of a difference in my life. Mother thinks Plantzilla is taking up too much of my time. I told them he needs me. They have been marking the days on the calendar until the end of the summer. I wish this summer with Plantzilla would never end. I think he feels that way, too.

Your student,
Mortimer

June 30

Dear Mr. Lester,
    Things got a little weird yesterday. The police think the robbery was an inside job. You have to tell Mother it has nothing to do with Plantzilla. She will listen to you. Grollier, her prizewinning Chihuahua, is gone. Mother shrieked and fainted when she found Grollier's diamond collar in Plantzilla's leaves. I told her maybe Grollier just went for a little walk.
        Please write to her and tell her that Plantzilla doesn't eat pets. She'll listen to you. She thinks I have been spending too much time with Plantzilla. She thinks I brush him too much. But I need to do these things. Plantzilla needs me.

        Mortimer

10 July

Dear Mr. Lester,

I felt I had to write to you. I knew of nowhere else to turn. If I had not seen these things with my own eyes, I would not have believed it: Plantzilla is able to move on its own! What is more, Plantzilla has developed an insatiable craving for meat — cooked meat of _any_ kind. I am worried about Mortimer. He has become very attached.

Although we are pleased to see Mortimer so motivated, Plantzilla has caused a great strain in our household. We Henrysons are not giver-uppers, but I am sure we are not the right family to continue with this program. I would be happy to have Plantzilla overnighted to you — at no cost to you at all, of course!

Very worriedly yours,
Mrs. Henryson

July 11

Mr. Lester,
Things have gotten worse. My parents wanted me to write to you. They are not happy at all. Last night at dinner they talked about putting Plantzilla out in the backyard until school starts. But Father is worried about the neighbors. I told them the pot roast was all my fault— Plantzilla was <u>so</u> hungry.

Mother is afraid for Grollier. I know he just went for a <u>very</u> long walk.

Could you write to them? I know they would listen to you. Tell them not to worry. Tell them to let Plantzilla stay. Father brought a shipping box home from his office. They want to send Plantzilla to you in the overnight mail. I don't think they can. Plus, Plantzilla doesn't want to go. PLEASE WRITE SOON AND EXPLAIN <u>EVERYTHING</u> TO THEM. HURRY!!

Mortimer

23 July

Dear Mr. Lester,

I am at a loss for where to begin. Events of this summer leave me quite baffled and searching for the proper way to put this. A metamorphosis has occurred in Plantzilla. He is no longer what he was. And we are not sure what he is turning out to be. Henry, Mr. Henryson, and I were wondering if it is ever possible for a plant to take on _human_ characteristics. I know this sounds more than strange, but we were wondering if a species such as Plantzilla might show feelings. Henry wonders if I may have offended Plantzilla — not taking part in grooming his cilia. Despite that, Plantzilla shows enormous caring for us.

In assessing these developments, we wonder if perhaps some of the causes of these _changes_ rest with our Mortimer. When we consider all of the time, careful attention, and nurturing he has lavished on Plantzilla, it leaves us with one conclusion alone: When you give a living thing love, you never know where it will lead. We have grown very attached to Plantzilla. Whatever will we do without him?

Very truly yours,
Mrs. Henry Henryson

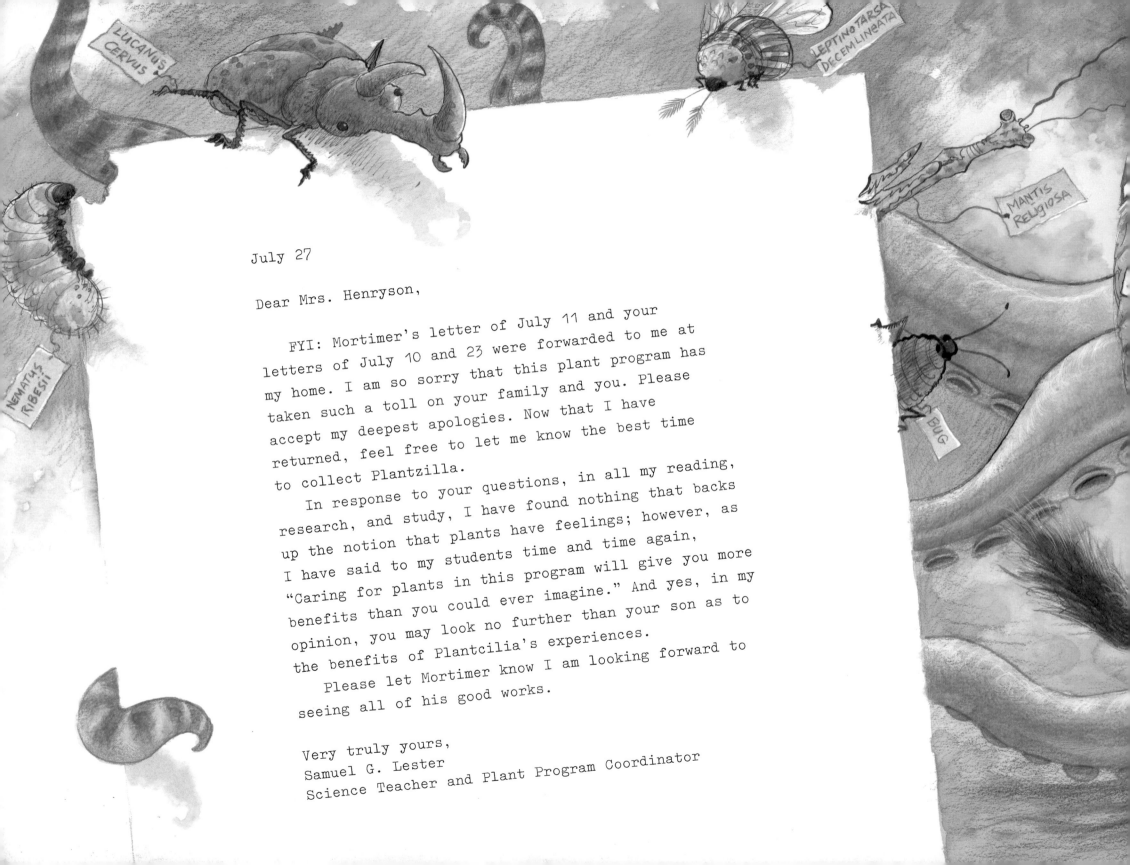

July 27

Dear Mrs. Henryson,

FYI: Mortimer's letter of July 11 and your
letters of July 10 and 23 were forwarded to me at
my home. I am so sorry that this plant program has
taken such a toll on your family and you. Please
accept my deepest apologies. Now that I have
returned, feel free to let me know the best time
to collect Plantzilla.

In response to your questions, in all my reading,
research, and study, I have found nothing that backs
up the notion that plants have feelings; however, as
I have said to my students time and time again,
"Caring for plants in this program will give you more
benefits than you could ever imagine." And yes, in my
opinion, you may look no further than your son as to
the benefits of Plantcilia's experiences.

Please let Mortimer know I am looking forward to
seeing all of his good works.

Very truly yours,
Samuel G. Lester
Science Teacher and Plant Program Coordinator

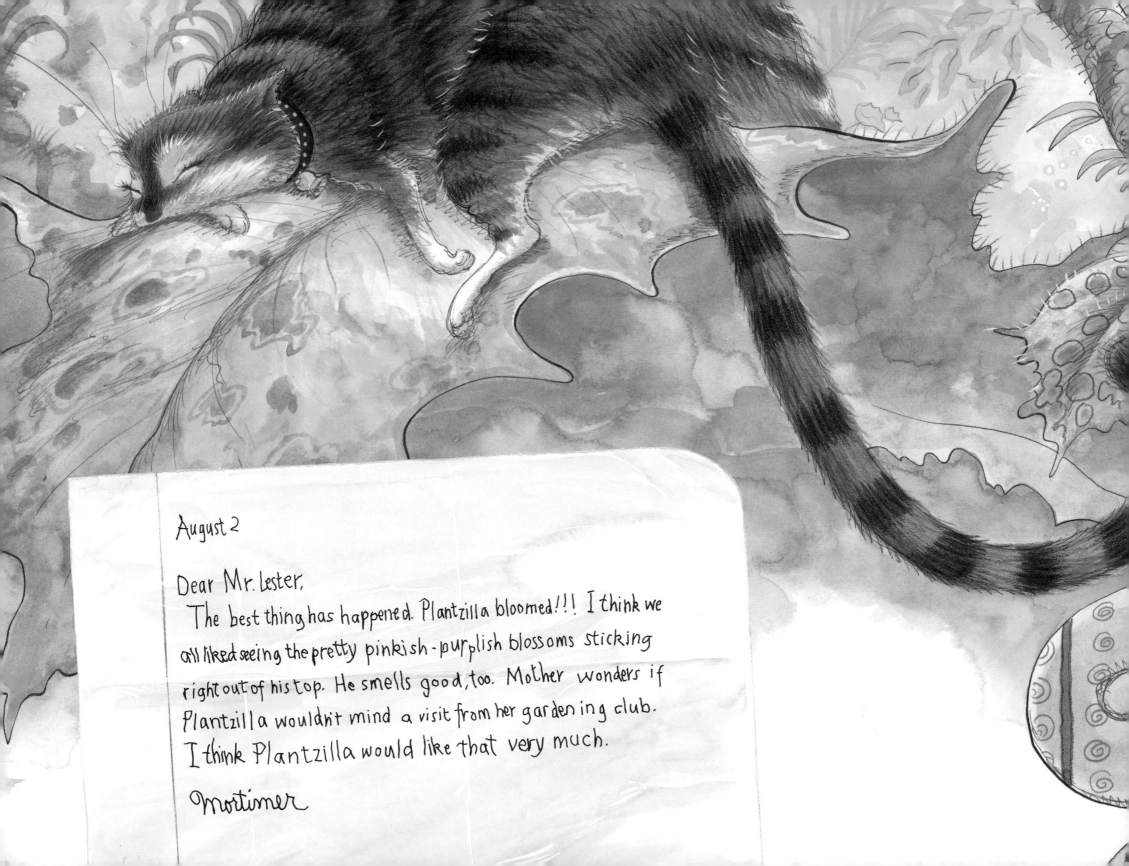

August 2

Dear Mr. Lester,
 The best thing has happened. Plantzilla bloomed!!! I think we all liked seeing the pretty pinkish-purplish blossoms sticking right out of his top. He smells good, too. Mother wonders if Plantzilla wouldn't mind a visit from her gardening club.
I think Plantzilla would like that very much.

Mortimer

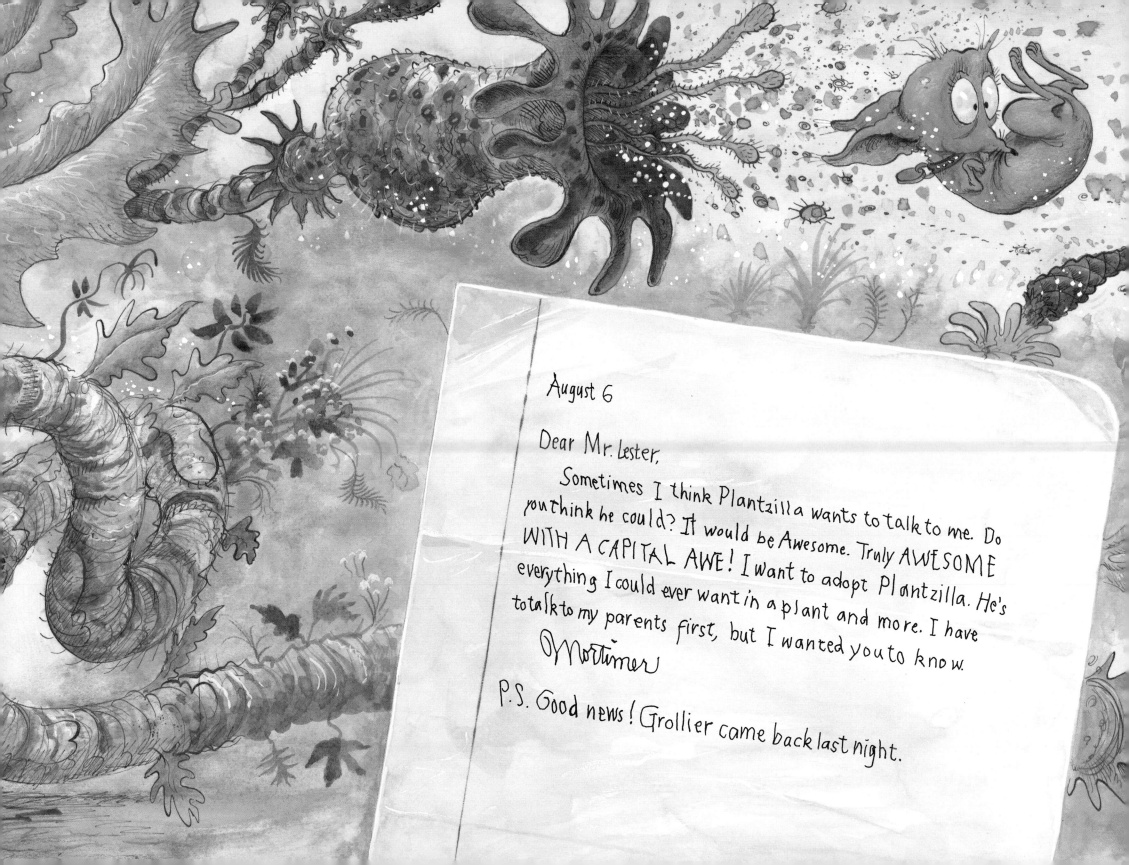

August 6

Dear Mr. Lester,
    Sometimes I think Plantzilla wants to talk to me. Do you think he could? It would be Awesome. Truly AWESOME WITH A CAPITAL AWE! I want to adopt Plantzilla. He's everything I could ever want in a plant and more. I have to talk to my parents first, but I wanted you to know.
                                    Mortimer

P.S. Good news! Grollier came back last night.

12 August

Dear Mr. Lester,

Mortimer was right all along! I do not know how we ever got along without Plantzilla. We would like it very much if Plantzilla could live with us forever. He is everything we could ever want in a plant, and more! Under the circumstances, I think it is the right thing to do.

Last night when we had a family meeting to discuss whether or not to adopt Plantzilla, we heard a great commotion coming from the part of the house where Plantzilla has taken his rooms. We rushed to him right away. There was nothing out of the ordinary, except the attached letter. We found it resting on Plantzilla's middle leaves. It seems to be addressed to you. We wonder if you could fill in some details, or perhaps you would just like to leave what is there between us and the paper it is written on.

Ever so sincerely yours in friendly hopefulness,
The Henry Henrysons

Attachment

11 Asugt.

Durr Lssstttʀ,

Tankk u. mii homɘ in this
pLaaz Nicɜ. Pɜɜɜple Goooo.D.
I wiL sta widdɘm
wɘ
fro Ɛvɘr!

PLLantxxciLia

August 14

Dear Mr. and Mrs. Henryson,

    In view of the circumstances, it would appear
that Plantzilla has found the perfect home!

Yours very truly,
Samuel G. Lester
Science Teacher and Plant Program Coordinator

P.S. Do please keep in touch.